Sandaara

ORBS Book 1

By Jo Carey

COPYRIGHT

ISBN 13: 978-1-948716-39-0

CHAPTER ONE

"Ben Thurgood, please report to the headmaster's office," flashed on my datapad. "NOW," appeared on the screen in red and yellow swirling bands. It was really tough to ignore, but I tried.

"You'd better go," my pal, Rufus, said. "If you get any more discipline chips, you'll be stuck here over the break. Then I'd have to party with all those hot Sandaaran chicks myself."

"I can't let that happen. After all, I'm an honorary Sandaaran. I must protect my people at all costs."

I stowed my datapad in my pack, and left Rufus to finish the report on our project by himself.

I was at the top of my class at LSI, the League's Statecraft Institute, a training school for those with exceptional IQ's and historical lineage. Rufus was further down the rankings. He had only been accepted at LSI because of his adoptive mother's role as head of the LPS Historical Council and his biological link to the Goranthi ruling class. He was half Goranthi, half elf, and all muscle. We met on our first day at LSI. Now that our program was almost complete, we were trying to have as much fun as possible before we have to face the world of expectations our families put on us. Rufus would have been happy to stay at LSI a bit longer, but I was ready to move on.

XXX

"Nice to see you again, Mr. Thurgood. It seems like only a few weeks since our last visit."

"It's nice to see you, Headmaster Lornick, but we really must stop meeting like this."

"Yes, well if you can hang on to your grade point average a few more months, neither of us will have to endure too many more of these impromptu chats."

"I am in a bit of a hurry, sir. I just finished my last class before the break. I'm heading to Sandaara for a job interview."

"Well, then I'll get right to the point. I'm sure you thought it was funny to reprogram the welcome instructions for visiting dignitaries."

"Actually, I did think the old instructions were a bit too stuffy. I felt sure you'd want our visitors to know that we have a relaxed and caring atmosphere here at LSI."

"Well, perhaps if the wife of the Sokuhl ambassador hadn't been well into her third century, I might have found your little prank less annoying. As it is, I doubt I will ever forget the sight of her walking down the ramp of the shuttle in her under garments."

"And I thought it was just humans that had an issue with modesty."

"Here," Lornick said, handing me a chip with my photo on it. "Put it in your box on the way out."

"I'm surprised you still have any of these laying around," I said, pocketing the chip. "I thought we used them all."

"I ordered a large supply after your first term here," Headmaster Lornick said, closing the door behind me.

CHAPTER TWO

"Ruf, I'm going to go start pre-flight," I said. "Get Sam and meet me on the Screamer. We launch in thirty." I grabbed by bag off the bed and headed for the docking bay where my ship, the Screamer, was docked. My mom wasn't happy when I brought the ship back with me after my last holiday, but Dad understood that a guy needs to be able to take off whenever the urge strikes. I love flying, I think Mom worries that I'll decide to be a pilot rather than taking some government council position where I sit in an office all day. She's right, but we never talk about it.

"Welcome back, sir. What is the plan for today?" Out asked.

"Please file a flight plan to Sandaara. Accept first available launch window at 30 minutes or more," Ben said. "Has there been anything unusual going on in my absence?"

"No, Ben. All is well."

"Thanks, Out." I smiled. My navigator is an advanced AI--a gift from my parents. He has a name, but it was too formal, so I just call him, Out. I smile every time we communicate.

I headed aft and stowed my gear. I'd never tell Mom this, but I felt like my cabin on the Screamer was home. I'd had the screamer since I was twelve and, over the years, Dad and I had made a lot of mods to her.

"Ben, Sam is requesting access through the main hatch. Rufus is with her," Out said over the speakers.

"Sure. Let 'em in so we can get underway, Out," I said, heading back to the cockpit.

"Your cabins are ready. Stow your gear. I'll meet you in the lounge once we jump to FTL," I said as I passed them on my way to the cockpit.

I've been flying ships since I was a kid--first with my dad and then on my own. I love the excitement of space travel. I've met people who never leave the planets they're born on and seem happy, but I enjoy exploring different planets and stations. You meet a lot of strange and interesting beings.

I was preparing for the FTL jump, when Out said I had an incoming transmission. "This is the PSS Screamer, Captain Thurgood at your service."

"Well, Captain Thurgood, did you think you could just sneak off to some party planet for your break and not tell me."

"Hello, Mom. How are you and Dad?"

"We're fine. You would know that if you bothered to come home and spend your school break with us."

"That's lame, Mom, and you know it. I love you guys, but I need to explore my options."

"Exactly what options are you exploring with this trip? Do you have a job interview?"

"Yes. I'm having some discussions about my possible future service."

"Service to whom?"

"The Sandaarans. I've been invited to meet with the Sandaaran Council."

"I wasn't aware of that. Are you seriously considering a role in Sandaaran government? I had hoped you'd take a position with the League, but the Sandaarans could certainly use someone with your familiarity with other League planets. It is awfully far away though."

"I'm just exploring options at this point. I don't have to make any decisions now. I'll let you know how it goes. Say hi to Dad."

"Stay safe and try not to get into any trouble. Sandaara is a remote place. Give our regards to Dram if you see him."

"I will. I'm sure he'll be at the interview." I love my mom, but she wants me to follow in her footsteps. She's now the

Chancellor of the Tralaskan Council. I'm proud of her, but I want to chart my own course. Dad gets it, but mom still holds out hope that I'll take an interest in politics at some level.

After the jump to FTL, I left Out running things and headed for the small lounge. "I can't believe we're spending our break on Sandaara," Sam said. "Have you ever been there, Ruf?"

"No. It's only been in the League as long as we've been alive, and it's pretty remote from the other planets."

Sam and Ruf are my best friends. We've known each other since we were toddlers. Are parents are all friends. Part of the problem with deciding on our future plans is that we want to stay together or at least find jobs that keep us in the same area.

"Are you really thinking of working for the Sandaaran government?" Sam asked.

"I have no idea what I want to do after school. I guess if I had to work in some government job at least the Sandaarans would be interesting, but there's got to be something more interesting we can do. Right?" My two best friends nodded, but I knew they didn't have the answer either. None of us wanted to take a boring job sitting behind a desk in some government office. That's what we were expected to do, but not what we wanted.

CHAPTER THREE

When I got the invite from Sandaara, it seemed like a great idea to make the trip our school break. I visited Sandaara a couple of times with my parents when I was younger. I was made an honorary Sandaaran because of a mission my parents were involved in when my Mom learned she was pregnant with me. Sandaarans are an ancient race that is a human avian hybrid.

"Sam, will it be weird to be on a planet where all the native population can fly?" Sam is half Basili and half Sokuhl. She has functional wings which is really awesome.

"I think it'll be cool. I've been to Nest, the Basili hidden city on Sokuhl, but this should be fun. You did say we're staying at a resort, right? I wonder if they'll be places designated for flying?"

"I'm not sure. Since they all fly, maybe they don't see the need to designate a special place for it. I don't remember much about my earlier visits. I know they fly outside the city, but I think when they're in the more populated areas they walk. I guess air traffic control was an issue. The resort's pretty new. It should be nice. You'll have your own room and Ruf can room with me."

"Out, we're out. Lock up the Screamer and set all the alarms. If you get lonely, give me a call."

"What about the guest in cabin D?"

"There's no one in cabin D, Out."

"Yes, there is."

"Why didn't you tell me someone was on the Screamer?"

"I thought she was your guest."

"She?" Sam asked. "Let's go meet this mystery woman."

"That would be me," a small high-pitched voiced said from the hall.

"Ophyllia, what the plark are you doing here?"

"Nobody wanted to spend their break hanging out with a kid." Ophyllia, was a 17-year-old uber smart student at LSI. Her IQ and her genetics were both exceptional.

"So, you decided to stow away on the Screamer," I said. "That's not cool, Phyl."

"I heard you were going to Sandaara. I've never been anywhere. I won't get in your way."

"Wait here," I told her, motioning for Ruf and Sam to follow me back to the hatch. "What are we gonna do?"

"She's here. There's not much we can do," Sam said.

Ophyllia walked up. "I can stay on the ship. I'll just go out every day and mingle with the population. Read a few souls. You know, scope out the local color. I'll be fine. I'm not a child, I'm seventeen and smarter than any of you."

"We know your IQ, Phyl, but we can't leave you on your own."

"Ben, I can look after Ms. Ophyllia," Out said. "Give her a tracer pendant so she can communicate with me when she leaves the ship. It's Sandaara. What can happen?"

"I seem to remember my mother being held hostage by these people at one point," Ben said.

"True but look how well it turned out. Your mother is now an advisor to the Sandaaran President. She didn't hold a grudge, so why should you?"

Ben went to the cockpit and returned with a small round ball on a leather strap. "Here. Wear this all the time. It allows you to communicate with Out. Stay out of trouble. There's plenty of food in the galley."

"I have credits. I can take care of myself," Phyl said.

"I'll be back to check on you," I told her as I cycled the hatch and walked out into the spaceport with my friends. Phyl was a good kid, but she was still a kid.

"You know she has a crush on you, right?" Sam asked as we made our way out of the Spaceport.

"Who?" I asked.

"Oblivious, as always," Sam laughed. "Phyl has a crush on you."

"Phyl just didn't want to spend the break at LSI, and I can't blame her for that," I said. Rufus elbowed me in the ribs, and I nearly ran into a guy walking beside us. I glared at Ruf, and he pointed to an attractive young woman with a sign that said "Welcome, Ben Thurgood."

I walked up to her and said, "I'm Ben Thurgood."

"Welcome, Mr. Thurgood. These must be your friends, Samantha Lawrence and Rufus Aymar-Scott. Please follow me."

I had no idea what was going on. I shrugged at my friends and followed. She was gorgeous. I'd probably follow her even if she didn't invite me to.

"We have a conveyance waiting to take you to the resort," she said. "My name is M'triska."

"Thanks. That wasn't necessary, but we appreciate it," I said. "So how did you get assigned to meet us?"

"I volunteered. I guess you could say I'm a fan."

"A fan of what?"

"Of you, Mr. Thurgood. You're something of a legend around here."

"I think you must have me confused with my father, Jason Thurgood. This is my third visit to your planet. The last time I was here I was maybe six years old."

"That's right. In school, we all learn about your parents' role in getting Sandaara to join the League."

"I'll let my father know he has fans here. He'll get a kick out of that."

We followed M'Triska to a vehicle where a young man was waiting. He loaded our luggage, and M'Triska motioned for us to take seats. The man was our driver, and our hostess sat with us and continued her story.

"It will take us a few minutes to reach the resort where you'll be housed during your visit, but I think you misunderstood me before. Many of the young people on Sandaara follow your... shall we say exploits, on First Contact."

"Well, don't believe everything you read," I said, not sure how I felt about having groupies.

"I hope I haven't upset you," she said. "I assumed you were aware that you are something of a role model to the youth of Sandaara. We all hope to be as brave, daring, and caring as Benjamin Thurgood."

"For the sake of all of us, please stop," Sam said. "He'll be impossible to live with."

"Oh, you two are living together? I'm sorry. I didn't know."

"No. Ben and I are definitely not living together, or dating, or anything," Sam said.

I thought her answer was just a little too quick.

"Well, in that case, I'd be happy to show you around while you're here, Ben. We're all hoping that you decide to take the job."

I was glad that we pulled up in front of our hotel then. I wasn't sure what the heck was going on, and I couldn't decide if I should be flattered, concerned, or creeped out.

CHAPTER FOUR

I had to be up early for my interview, but I still hit snooze a few times before finally getting out of bed and heading to the shower. My original idea in accepting this interview wasn't so much that I thought I might actually want the job, but I thought Sandaara was remote enough to allow me to get my first interview out of the way without everyone I know hearing all the details. M'Triska's comments made me think I might have underestimated the Sandaarans continuing interest in my family.

"Message us when you're done," Ruf said without opening his eyes. "Good luck, I guess."

"Thanks. I think I'll go check on Phyl after I finish. I still feel like we shouldn't have left her on her own."

"If there was an issue, Out would have called. Phyl's fine. She just tries too hard to fit in."

XXX

Phyl spent her first night on Sandaara researching the spaceport and surrounding area online. With her pink backpack slung over one shoulder, she headed for the hatch. "Out, I'm out."

"No. I'm out," he said.

"Yes, you are, and so am I."

"Where are you headed, Ms. Ophyllia?"

"I thought I'd take in a couple of the museums and maybe do some shopping."

"Be sure you have your pendant. I'd appreciate it if you'd check in now and then in case Ben calls and wants to know how you're doing."

"Ben Thurgood has probably already forgotten I'm here."

"I'm sure that's not true."

"It's OK. I'm used to it. It's just my life at this point. I don't let it bother me."

"Just the same, I'd appreciate a check in now and then. You have fun."

"I plan on it," she said and closed the hatch behind her. She headed out of the spaceport and into the city. It was exciting to see so many people with wings. The Sandaarans were different. In the heart of the city, they walked everywhere, but it was interesting to see how their clothing accommodated their wings.

XXX

"Good morning, Mr. Thurgood," M'Triska said, as I walked out the front door of the resort. "If you'll settle in, I'll see that you get to your appointment with time to spare."

Although I knew that I didn't want to be a government worker for any government, at least not until I was too old to do something more exciting, I knew I needed to make a good impression or my mom would be on my case. It's funny, she has a special kinship with the Sandaarans although it's my dad that carries the Sandaaran genes in his DNA. I pulled out my datapad and reviewed the messages I exchanged with Councilor Dram about the interview. He hadn't talked about a job title or provided any details. I'd just have to wing it. I'm cool with that.

"Are you excited about your interview?" M'Triska asked.

"Sure."

"You must have so many opportunities. How are you going to choose?"

"I'm still working that out."

The vehicle stopped in front of a large office building. "The council offices are on the fifteenth floor. Check in at the security desk when you get inside."

"Thanks," I said as I grabbed my datapad. I wondered if M'Triska would be waiting for me when I was finished. It's funny, I've been in a lot of government buildings on many planets of the League when my Mom took me with her when I was younger. They all look alike. There were subtle differences most of which I probably missed. Subtle isn't really my style. I noticed that all the buildings on Sandaara seemed to be tall. Maybe it's because they can fly. I wished Dad's DNA had passed along that ability.

I approached a window labeled security. "Mr. Thurgood, welcome to Sandaara. We hope you'll decide to join our government," the guard said. He handed me a pendant. "Just wear this when you're in the building. Take the elevators to the fifteenth floor."

When I exited the lift, an older woman approached. "Mr. Thurgood, welcome back to Sandaara. Councilor Dram is waiting for you. Please follow me."

She showed me to a seat and sat down behind a large desk. I'd only been waiting a couple of minutes when the inner office door opened and a large Sandaaran male walked toward me with his hand extended.

"Benjamin Thurgood, welcome back. I hope perhaps someday soon I'll be able to say welcome home." I stood and shook his hand. "Follow me," he said.

He asked about my parents, and I shared their current projects.

"I was pleased to hear that your mother is now the leader of the Tralaskan Council, I only hope she'll still find time to visit us again soon."

"I'm sure she will."

I reminded Counselor Dram of my remaining time at school and tried to steer the conversation to the reason for the meeting.

"I'm sure you'd like to hear some details about the position we'd like you to consider," he said. "We realize that you are just finishing your studies at LSI. We've followed your progress for years."

I wasn't too comfortable with all these people telling me they'd been keeping tabs on me. I suspect he intended it to be a compliment, but it was just creepy.

CHAPTER FIVE

Phyl was enjoying the freedom of being on her own. Her exceptional IQ always meant that she was in classes with kids several years older than her. Things improved when she went to LSI. With a student body that included representatives of most League species, the students took classes based on their levels not their chronological age. If people accepted her in spite of her IQ, they often freaked when they learned that she was half earth human and half Venlanten Royal. Less than one percent of matings between those two species resulted in a child with Venlanten Royal DNA being dominate. Yep, Phyl was one special girl, and she hated it.

For her day of exploring, she dressed like a normal 17-year-old Earth Human. She was wearing a print skirt that hit her at mid-thigh, a pink t-shirt with a cute kitten on the front, and sneakers. Her dark glasses hid her Venlanten eyes. She had the pendant that linked her to Out around her neck, and her dangling earrings were metallic orbs she made herself. They were air content sensors, but she liked them because they were sparkly.

She enjoyed walking around on her own. Like her classmates at LSI, she'd be finishing her program in the next few months and had no idea what to do next. Her parents expected her to come home and take her place in the lower ranks of the powerful Venlanten Council. She wasn't ready for that. Not that she couldn't handle the work. That wouldn't be a problem, but it wasn't what she wanted to do.

She visited the Sandaaran National Museum and enjoyed seeing how people reacted to her when they didn't know anything about her. It was a little surreal to walk through the exhibit devoted to Ben's parents and the part of Sandaaran history they had discovered before Ben was born. Ben, Rufus, and Sam were her only real friends at LSI. She knew they didn't really want to be her friend, but they were all too nice to ignore her when she wormed her way into their group.

She only covered half the museum by lunch time, so she checked in with Out, and ate lunch at a cafe beside one of the pools in front of the museum. Now that Sandaara was welcoming visitors from throughout the League, the main government area had undergone a complete rebuild and now featured a series of pools where residents and visitors could splash in the water. The pools were lined with cafes, bars, and boutiques. Phyl liked to watch people, so she found a seat on the patio and ordered a sandwich and a porchiss berry cooler. Her drink came in a glass shaped like a lily. The museum's cafe featured fruit and flower-based drinks popular with Sandaarans, all of them served in glasses shaped like various flower blossoms.

A young couple sat at the bar, drinking. Phyl wondered if she'd ever have a boyfriend. She hoped so, and she thought as she got older her age wouldn't be such a big deal. She had a crush on Ben, but he didn't even seem to realize it. He still thought of her as just a kid, but he always looked out for her. Right now, her friends were all older, and they treated her like a little sister. Phyl took a seat on a high stool at the center of the bar, so she could watch the bartender pour drinks. She sipped her drink and listened to the conversations around her.

After she finished her lunch, she checked in with Out, and headed back into the museum. She planned to spend the afternoon in the natural history wing. When she checked out the museum's page on the interweb she saw that they were offering a special behind the scenes tour that allowed participants to see how specimens were prepared for display in the museum.

Always interested in the "how" of things, she'd signed up for the afternoon tour.

She met her tour group in the rotunda of the building. Their tour guide was an older Sandaaran who wore thick glasses. Everyone introduced themselves and followed along behind the guide who had said to call him "professor." The first stop was the receiving bay. Professor pointed out various crates and containers and explained the different ways artifacts were transported to the museum. Sandaarans hadn't really embraced their history until Dr. Nebulon Blyst, Ben's mother, visited the planet and solved some mysteries that allowed the Sandaarans to embrace their past and become active members of the League of Planetary Systems.

Most of those on the tour were young Sandaarans. "You're from Earth, right?" a young Sandaaran male asked.

"Yes. I study at LSI," Phyl said.

"I'm Tren," he said.

"Nice to meet you Tren. My name is Phyl."

They turned their attention back to Professor as he explained the next stop on their tour. "We're very lucky. Today Dr. Brusher will be unpacking some scrolls sent to us from the Museum of the Ancient Americans on Earth. Phyl, are you familiar with that institution?"

"Certainly. It's one of the most prestigious museums of ancient history on Earth," she said.

"We believe these scrolls contain glyphs which will provide further proof that the ancient Sandaarans traveled extensively throughout our universe. It's very exciting. You're very lucky to have chosen today to take this tour. Let's step behind the line, and watch this historic moment unfold."

Phyl stood beside Tren and watched as a sealed environmental chamber was wheeled in and placed beside a work bench where an older Sandaaran male in a white lab coat waited anxiously, his gloved hands visibly trembling in excitement. "The scroll will be photographed from every possible angle. It will be thoroughly measured, every possible nondestructive test will be run on all the materials, and then it will be placed in an environmental wrapper so that it can be safely displayed."

The assembled tour group and lab personnel held their collective breaths as the case was opened. "What the plark?" Phyl said, causing everyone to turn and glare at her.

CHAPTER SIX

"What's wrong with you?" Tren asked.

"Professor, if that scroll is genuine it would have been shipped in a sealed crate filled with porlumin gas. Opening the crate would have caused all the humanoid species in the room to pass out immediately."

"Are you an expert on artifact restoration, Miss?" Professor asked.

"No, but I've done extensive research, and I know how these things work," Phyl said. "That scroll is a fake, and he must be in on it," she said, pointing a finger at the white-coated scientist.

"Get her out of here. It's urgent that we get this scroll photographed, measured, and into its protective sleeve as quickly as possible. A look passed between the scientist and the tour guide.

Two security guards stepped up on either side of Phyl, and took her arms moving her out of the lab. "Let go of me," she yelled. "This is crazy. I'm just telling you that someone is selling you fake artifacts. You should be thanking me," Phyl yelled as security hustled her through the back hallways of the museum trying to keep her out of public view.

They deposited her in a small office with a table and a chair. "Hand over your backpack and communicator," one of the guards said.

"You have no right to take my stuff," Phyl said.

They took her stuff, walked out, and closed the door behind them. She tried the door, but it was locked. She plopped down in the chair and replayed the events in the lab. She figured some museum administrator would come in to talk to her about disrupting the tour. They might ban her from the museum, but that was about all they could do.

As she waited, she remembered she had the comm pendant from Ben's ship.

"Out, this is Phyl."

"Hi, Ms. Ophyllia. Are you enjoying the museum?"

"It's been interesting. If I send you a sensor file can you analyze it?"

"Sure. What kind of sensor?"

"Gas."

"Are you in some kind of trouble, Ms. Ophyllia?"

"No. I'm enjoying a behind the scenes tour of the museum. It's quite interesting. I have a really strong sense of smell and thought there might be a small gas leak. Can you check it for me?"

"Will do, Ms. Ophyllia."

"Thanks, Out."

Phyl had no idea how long she'd been sitting in the room, but she was bored. She wasn't worried about her situation, so she used the marker board on the wall to work out some design changes for a new tracker device she was working on.

She got lost in the work and didn't know if she'd been waiting a few minutes or a few hours, but the amount of information on the board indicated she'd been there for some time before the door opened and an attractive young Sandaaran male entered. He set her backpack and communicator on the table.

"Ophyllia Devlin. Such a pretty name with such a powerful legacy," he said.

Phyl stopped writing on the board and turned to face him. "And you are?"

"Here to find out why you disrupted our tour."

"I didn't disrupt your tour. I exclaimed when I saw your lab person open an environmental chamber that should have contained a dangerous gas."

"And you know this how?"

"I'm very smart. I know a lot of things about a lot of things."

He eyed the calculations on the board. "Yes. I can see that. Why are you here Ms. Devlin?"

"I'm here on holiday with some of my friends from LSI."

"Were you're friends on the tour with you?"

"No. Ben had an interview with your government today, and the others were at the resort."

He set his forearms on the table and said nothing for a few minutes. "Explain to me what you think you saw in the lab."

With an exasperated sigh, Phyl explained again about how the scroll should have been protected during shipment and how releasing the gas would have affected everyone in close proximity. "The scroll was not properly protected during shipment. That means that you were sold a fake that didn't need to be protected. It also means that your scientist knew there wasn't dangerous gas in that crate, so he must be in on it."

"You think we've been duped?"

"I couldn't really say whether you were involved or not, though by the way you're looking at me now, I'm going to guess that you are aware that some, maybe even all of the artifacts on display in this museum are fakes."

She watched his pupils dilate and his hands clinch into fists. "I'm afraid your letting your imagination get the best of you, Ms. Devlin. I can assure you that this museum only purchases artifacts that have been appropriately vetted. I've read your file, and it seems you're prone to pointing out flaws that are just a figment of your overactive imagination. Here," he said, holding out her backpack for her to slip her arms through the straps. "I'll escort you out."

"I didn't catch your name," she said.

That was it. He didn't ask any more questions and didn't ban her from the museum though she suspected her photo would be circulated to the security team. She walked away from the museum and stopped at a small stand selling drinks by one of the pools. She bought a porchiss berry cooler served in a tulip shaped glass and sat down to gather her thoughts. Her communicator buzzed silently. She read Out's report. The breakdown matched the typical readings for Sandaara, just as she suspected it would. She sent Out a thank you message just as Tren approached.

"Are you OK? What did they do to you?"

"They stuck me in an office while they pulled up my file. Did I miss anything of interest on the rest of the tour?"

"You were the most interesting thing on the tour," Tren said, causing Phyl to blush. "Do you mind if I get a drink and join you?"

"I'd like that." She watched him as he walked up to the bar and ordered a drink. Another young man approached him and said something to Tren before walking away.

They guy looked familiar but Phyl didn't think much about it after Tren returned to the table.

CHAPTER SEVEN

"How did it go?" Sam asked when I called.

"Interesting, I guess. Did you and Ruf already eat?"

"Yeah. We got hungry. What took so long?"

"They took me out to dinner. Can we have drinks and dissect this?"

"Sure. I'll get Ruf and meet you in the lobby in a few minutes."

M'Triska had not been the one to drive me back to the resort. Once my interview was finished, Dram took me out to dinner with other members of the ruling council. When we finished, I was driven back to the resort by an older man who didn't speak to me at all. I appreciated the quiet. Dram had given me a lot of information and there was more discussion during dinner. I knew I wasn't going to take the job, but I needed to come up with a way to say no and still stay in the Sandaarans' good graces, as well as my mom's.

I took a quick shower and threw on jeans and a t-shirt, grabbing my pilot's jacket on the way out the door. Ruf and Sam were waiting for me when I stepped off the elevator. "There's a nice little place not far from here. We can walk," Sam said. "It must be cool to be able to fly everywhere."

"I'd probably drop out of the sky," Rufus said. "This body isn't really streamlined for flight."

We all laughed as we walked to the cafe. It was a small place offering beverages from around the League. I ordered a black coffee from Earth, Sam had her usual Venecian tea, and Rufus had some fruity drink that came in one of those flower blossom shaped glasses that the Sandaarans seemed to favor.

"Should we be checking out the local job options?" Rufus asked as we sat down at a table near the windows.

"Only if you're trying to get away from me," I said.

"Not your dream job?" Sam asked.

I explained about my interview with Dram and then dinner with the other government types. "They want me to be their trade attaché. Basically, I'd be negotiating trade agreements with other League and non-League planets. Until my mom came here, the Sandaarans hadn't traveled or interacted with their neighbors in space. Since joining the League, they're working to change not only their image but the affect it has on the progress of their civilization."

Sam and Rufus got into a discussion of whether or not I'd be a good trade attaché. "It doesn't matter, guys. While I'm pleased that they would offer me a job that is so important to the future of their planet, it's not what I want to do."

"Did you check on Phyl today?" Sam asked.

"Crap. I meant to, but I forgot. I was going to stop by the ship before I headed back to the resort, but the dinner thing threw me off." I stepped under a commbrella and pulled out my communicator. "Out, is everything OK there?"

"All is well, Ben. How did the interview go?"

"It was OK. How's Phyl?"

"Last time she checked in, she seemed to be enjoying herself."

"When was that?"

"It was several hours ago."

"Plark. She shouldn't be roaming around alone this late. I'll call her. Thanks, Out."

I walked back to the table and motioned for Sam and Rufus to follow me. "Phyl's not on the ship," I told them. "I called, but she didn't answer. She shouldn't be out alone this late in a strange place. I don't think she has the best people skills. I'm going to get my datapad. I can't believe I forgot all about her."

"She's not your responsibility, Ben," Sam said.

"She was on my ship. I'm the captain. She's my responsibility whether she was supposed to be there or not. Grab your datapads and whatever you need. We're going to need a vehicle."

"Call M'Triska. She might have access to a vehicle," Sam suggested.

"It's kind of late. This problem hasn't got anything to do with my interview."

"She'll help."

"How can you be so sure?"

"God, it amazes me that you can still be this clueless. She likes you."

I gave her a look that made it clear I didn't understand.

"You know, like boyfriend material. Call her."

I looked to Rufus to back me up, but he shrugged his giant shoulders and headed for our room.

CHAPTER EIGHT

I went to the room, dumped out by backpack and threw in my datapad and other stuff I thought might be useful. I pulled out M'Triska's card and punched her code into my communicator.

"Hi, M'Triska. It's Ben Thurgood. I'm sorry to call so late."

"Hi, Ben. How did your interview go?"

"I think it went well, but I need your help with something."

"Sure, Ben. What can I do?"

"Do you have access to a vehicle?"

"I can arrange to use one of the government vehicles tomorrow, if you'd like to take a tour."

"I need a vehicle tonight. We need to find a friend of ours who's in the city. We have a way to track her whereabouts, but we need to catch up to her quickly."

"Is she in some kind of trouble?"

"I hope not. I'll fill you in on all the details when you get here. Can you get a vehicle and pick us up?"

"I'll do it. See you as quick as I can get there."

I was surprised. Maybe Sam was onto something after all. I did get the impression that although Sandaarans were now allowed to travel, must of them still didn't. It seemed like the young people were curious about the outside world but not yet ready to explore it on their own. "*Wow, I sound like a grown up. When did that happen?*" I wondered as I headed out the door to meet my friends.

"M'Triska will be here soon. Out can track Phyl with the comm pendant. I just hope she doesn't get herself into trouble before we can catch up with her."

Rufus and Sam both told me not to worry, but I worried anyway. I didn't like it. Responsibility was never something I enjoyed and being responsible for another person was definitely not on my list of ways to spend my break from LSI.

"Ben, this is Out."

"Yeah, Out. Did Phyl come back?"

"No. I got a message from her with a sensor data file attached. She asked me to analyze the file but said not to talk to her over the comm, but to send a message. She said she was going to dinner with a friend."

"At least that should mean she's staying put for a while. That should give us a chance to get to her location. We're just waiting for our ride," I explained, feeling a little less crazed than before.

"Any idea what's in the file she sent?"

"There was nothing. I sent her the results. She said it was what she expected."

Just as I finished talking to Out and explained what was happening to Sam and Rufus, M'Triska pulled up in a vehicle that looked like it was used to make some kind of deliveries. It was painted bright green with pink polka dots. I opened the door, and we all climbed in.

"Thanks for this, M'Triska," I said as I climbed into the front passenger seat. "A young girl that goes to school with us at LSI stowed away on my ship. Now, she's out roaming around the city, and we need to find her."

"Oh my. That's terrible. I'm sure she'll be fine. We have a very low crime rate here. Will she be scared?"

"Probably not," Sam said. "That's part of the problem. She looks older than she is, and she's not used to being around a lot of people she doesn't know."

I opened my datapad and pulled up the data from Phyl's pendant. I overlaid a map of the city. "She's moving along the civic pools."

"Great," M'Triska said as she drove us into the heart of the city. "We'll park at the closest spot and track her down on foot. There are no vehicles allowed on the Pool Esplanade."

CHAPTER NINE

"What did you see in the lab back there that made you blurt that stuff out?" Tren asked when he returned with his drink. "The guide and the scientist both seemed pretty upset after security carted you off."

"That's probably because they're both in on it."

"In on what exactly?"

Phyl explained how she knew that the article was mishandled. "You think some people who work for the museum are buying fake artifacts and pocketing the money?" Tren asked.

"Yeah, and the administrator is in on it too. I suspect many of the items on display are fakes. Most people wouldn't be able to tell. I only noticed because of the gas."

"So, what are you going to do about it?"

"I hadn't thought about that. I guess I should report it."

"You just did," Tren said, pulling out a mini-datapad and laying it on the table in front of her. Phyl's eyes went wide as she read the information on the screen.

"You're a detective?" she asked.

"Shush. Keep it down. I'm under cover."

"You work for Sandaaran Security? You seem awfully young."

"And you seem awfully young to know so much about handling ancient artifacts."

Tren suggested they should probably put more space between them and the museum. He invited Phyl to have dinner with him, and they walked along the pools until they came to a small restaurant.

"I've been working on this case for a long time," he explained over dinner. "We know the museum is getting fake artifacts. We think the real things are being purchased with museum funds, then fakes are substituted for the real objects, so the real ones can be sold on the black market."

"I can tell you for sure after today that the tour guide, the guy in the lab coat, and the administrator are involved. I'm not sure how many others."

While they ate, they discussed ways to detect which artifacts on display were fake. "How long will you be on Sandaara?" Tren asked as they left the restaurant.

"Just for a few days, but let me know if I can help you with your case?"

As they walked along the civic pools, Tren took Phyl's hand. "Where are you staying?"

"Close to the spaceport," Phyl said, trying to be cautious. They stopped by one of the pools and sat down on a bench.

"I'm sorry for the way you were treated today," Tren said. "Please don't think badly of all Sandaarans because of your experience."

"Phyl, what are you doing," Ben asked as he walked up to the bench where Phyl was seated beside Tren. "I was worried about you."

"Yeah, we all were," Sam said as she joined the group followed by Rufus.

"As you can see, I'm just fine."

"So it seems," Sam said. "Who's your friend?"

"I'm Detective Tren Lurance of the Sandaaran Security Force. You're Ben Thurgood, aren't you? I heard you were going to be in town this weekend. It's an honor to meet you." Ben and Tren shook hands, and the rest of the group introduced themselves.

"Did Phyl get into some kind of trouble, Detective?"

"Not at all. In fact, she's been helping me with a case. Can I buy you all a drink? I'm afraid Phyl got a bad introduction to Sandaara. I can't have you all thinking badly of us. We're all hoping you'll take the job, Ben," Tren said, putting an arm around Ben's shoulder as he led them to a beverage bar further along the esplanade.

"Is he for real?" Sam asked Phyl as they followed along behind Tren.

"I'll never get a chance to find out," Phyl said. She thought Tren was flirting with her, and she was enjoying it, until her friends showed up.

They found a table and Tren and Ben headed to the bar to get drinks for everyone. "What did he mean when he said you didn't have a good introduction to Sandaara?" Sam asked.

"We might as well wait until they come back, so I don't have to tell it twice," Phyl said.

When the guys returned to the table and handed out the drinks, Tren said. "Your friend caused a bit of a stir at the Sandaaran History Museum today."

Phyl explained what happened and answered the questions the group asked. "So you think there's a group of people at the museum who are switching real artifacts for good quality fakes so they can sell the real thing on the black market and pocket the credits. Is that it?" Ben asked.

"So it seems. I've had them under surveillance for a while, but now I know at least three of those involved. It's been great meeting you all," Tren said, "but I have a ton of forms to file about all of this. Can I have your number, Phyl? We can meet tomorrow, so I can get your official statement."

Phyl hadn't been paying much attention as she did what she always did--melted into the background. Sam elbowed her in the side. "Give him your comm code," Sam said.

Phyl handed over a card with her comm code, and Tren stood to leave. "Want to walk me out?" he asked, extending his hand to Phyl. She took it and they walked out the front door of the cafe.

"Aw, that's sweet. Phyl's made a new friend," Rufus said.

"Yeah, she's doing better than the rest of us," Sam said, looking at M'Triska who had her armed wrapped around Ben's bicep.

"I'll call you tomorrow," Tren said, tucking a piece of hair behind Phyl's ear. "Maybe we can meet for lunch. Your friends are welcome to come along."

Phyl turned and walked back inside. "Everything OK?" Sam asked.

"Fine. Just fine," Phyl said. "Can I go back to the ship now?"

"Let's go get your things. You can stay with me at the resort," Sam said.

"I'd rather just stay on the ship. I'm settled in, and I like being on my own."

"We'll take you back to the spaceport then, but you've got to stay out of trouble," I said.

CHAPTER TEN

I insisted on walking Phyl back to the Screamer, so I could make sure she was in for the night. "Can I come along?" M'Triska asked. "I'd love to see your ship."

"Sure, I guess."

"Let's all go," Sam said, pulling Rufus out of the back seat.

"Why do I have to come?" he grumbled.

"I want company," Sam said, wrapping her arm around Rufus bulging bicep mimicking the way M'Triska was hanging onto Ben.

"Hi, Out. We're back," I called as we walked through the hatch. M'Triska had a death grip on my arm. I peeled her hands off once we were inside the ship.

"Hi, Ben and friends."

"Give me a tour, Ben," M'Triska said.

"Sam, can you show M'Triska around. I want to have a chat with Phyl."

"Sure thing. M'Triska follow me," Sam said, looking much too pleased with the assignment. Women. I'll never understand them. I went to the unused cabin, which I assumed was where Phyl had made herself at home. I opened the door and stepped back, motioning for her to enter.

"Sit down, Phyl," I said.

"Look Ben, I didn't do anything wrong. I didn't get into any trouble really. I just noticed something wasn't right and spoke up."

"I know, Phyl. You did good, but sometimes people aren't happy when you point out what they're doing wrong. If these guys thought you posed a threat, you could have been in big trouble."

"Not really. Tren was there."

"But you didn't know who he was until later."

"I had the comm pendant. I could have called Out.

"I know all that, but you still took some chances. You're a passenger on my ship, Phyl. You're my responsibility. My mother would kill me if I let anything happen to you."

"Your mother doesn't know me."

"Trust me, it wouldn't matter. Just promise me you'll be more cautious. By the way, be cautious of Detective Lurance too. I think he's interested. He's too old for you, Kid. He might not know that, but you do."

"Right. I'll be a good little girl. Can I meet him for lunch tomorrow and give my official statement?"

"Sure. You have to help the local police if you can, but don't put yourself in any danger. OK?"

"OK."

I gave her a friendly hug and closed the door behind me.

"Out."

"Yes, Ben."

"Keep an eye on her. Let me know when she leaves and track her movements would you?"

"Certainly, Ben."

I rounded up the rest of the gang and cycled the hatch. "Out, we're out. Have a good night."

M'Triska drove us back to our resort. As soon as she pulled up in front, Sam couldn't get out of the vehicle fast enough. "Come on, Ruf. What are you waiting for?" she asked.

"What's the rush?" Ruf asked. I saw Sam nod toward the front seats where M'Triska, and I were sitting. "Thank you for coming to our rescue," I said. “I really appreciate it."

"I'm glad. I can drive you wherever you want to go tomorrow," she said. "I could take you to the caves your mom discovered. Everyone can come along, or it could just be the two of us," she said.

"Thanks for the offer, but I think we're just going to hang out here at the hotel. I need to think about the position I discussed with Counselor Dram."

"If you change your mind, call me," she said before she drove away.

CHAPTER ELEVEN

Rufus always works out in the morning. I heard him leave but went back to sleep. I hadn't really made any plans for my stay on Sandaara, so I thought I'd hang out by the pool at the resort and check out the locals. Maybe drink was of those things served in a flower and figure out how long I could put off making a decision about my future.

My comm unit sounded before Rufus got back from the physical fitness room. "Morning, Sam. I want to sleep."

"You did sleep. Now it's time to wake up. Is Rufus back yet?"

"No. If you want to talk to Ruf, why did you call me?"

"Get your butt out of bed and get in the shower so Rufus can do the same when he gets back. I'll meet you both in the restaurant in an hour."

"Yes, mother." Sam was gorgeous and lots of times when we were out, people assumed she and I were a couple. You know--romantically. I was up for the idea, but Sam only had eyes for Rufus though he didn't seem to know that, and I hadn't yet decided how to tell him. I figured as we got older, he'd eventually figure it out, or she'd get tired of waiting for that to happen and tell him herself. Either way, my relationship with Sam was more like brother and sister though she did tend to mother me sometimes.

Since I was now completely awake, I couldn't find any reason not to do as Sam ask, so I had just finished packing my backpack when Rufus walked in. "Are we meeting Sam for breakfast?" he asked.

"Yeah. You've got twenty minutes," I told him as I pulled out my comm pendant. "Morning, Out. How are things on the Screamer?"

"All is quiet, Ben. Ms. Ophyllia is still sleeping."

"Make sure she calls me before she leaves."

"Will do. I have some routine system maintenance scheduled for today. Have a good day."

"Thanks, Out."

XXX

When Ruf was ready, we headed downstairs to meet Sam. She was waiting for us in the lobby. "Let's get some food. I'm starving," Ruf said.

"How can you possibly eat that much food?" Sam asked as Rufus set his plate on the table.

"It's a buffet. Did you expect me to eat like a bird just because we're on Sandaara?" Ruf smiled at his own joke.

"Good one," she said. "What's on tap for today?"

"I thought we'd just hang out by the pool. Relax, you know."

The look she gave me indicated I should have known better than to even suggest such a radical thing. "What?"

"We are on one of the most remote planets in the League, surrounded by a species that few of our classmates even know exist, and you want to hang by the pool."

"Yeah. I need some time to figure out how to tell my mom I'm not accepting this job so she agrees it's a good idea."

"Yeah," Ruf said. "We really do need to figure out a plan for after graduation. My folks will have me in a necktie before I even unpack."

"Lucky for your two, I have the perfect solution. Something interesting we can do that will give you plenty of time to think," Sam said. "Call M'Triska. Let's go to the caves your mom discovered."

"Really. That's how you want to spend our vacation?" I asked.

"Yes. We'll get to see more of the planet, and you'll get to spend more time with M'Triska. Will that be so horrible?"

"She is a little clingy."

"You love the hero worship vibe and you know it," she said. "Call her and set it up."

"I'm not sure I want..."

"Just think of the bonus points this will get you with your mom--taking an interest in her work and your heritage. It'll soften the blow of you declining the Sandaarans' job offer."

I shrugged. She made a good point. I walked outside onto the patio and pulled out my communicator. M'Triska was excited to take us to the caves. Apparently, Dram expected I might want to visit the site, so all the arrangements had been made before I arrived. I walked back to the table.

"She'll be here in in thirty minutes." I grabbed my cup and took a last gulp of coffee. "Should we take Phyl with us?"

"She has a lunch date, remember?" Sam said.

"Date? I don't think it's a date," I said.

"You're not her dad," Sam said. "She has a lunch date with a very attractive detective."

"She has to give her statement about what she saw at the museum yesterday," Rufus said. "You wouldn't want her to skip out on her civic duty, would you?"

"You're right. It'll just be the four of us."

"Don't worry, Ben. I'll protect you from the hot bird girl," Rufus said. "I'll take her off your hands if you want me to."

"No, you won't," Sam said, smacking his massive forearm.

"Ouch," he said. "That hurt."

"Right," Sam said. "Let's go, boys. We've got some exploring to do."

CHAPTER TWELVE

We were waiting when M'Triska pulled up in front of the hotel. "I'm so excited you decided to make the trip to the caves," she said. "It'll be a long day, but a fun one. I've got plenty of food and water in the back."

I held back hoping that Sam or Rufus would take the front passenger seat beside M'Triska, but they climbed into the back so I had no choice. It wasn't that I minded the attention of a beautiful woman. I could handle that, but M'Triska seemed to know a lot about me, and that was kind of creepy. I know you can go on FirstContact and find tons of personal info on anyone in the League these days, but it seemed wrong and made her feel more like a stalker than someone I might want to date.

As we drove, Sam pulled up information about my mom's discovery of the caves and the monument that had been built there. She read the account out loud with M'Triska adding comments here and there. "Did you go to the caves when you were here with your Mom before?" Sam asked.

"No. We went to the opening of a display in the museum, and she had a bunch of meetings," I said. "That's all I remember."

We were just leaving the city when my comm bleeped. "Go for Ben."

"Hi, Ben. It's Phyl. Out said you wanted me to check in."

"You doing OK this morning?"

"I'm fine."

"What are your plans for the day?"

"I want to do some research online and see if I can come up with anything that will help Tren with his investigation.

"Weren't your Mom and Dad involved in stopping the sale of black-market artifacts?"

"I think so. That was back before I was born. I'm not sure they'd know any of the current players."

"Would it be OK, if I suggest to Tren that he message your mom to see if she could be of any help?"

"That's a great idea. I'm sure she'd love to help the Sandaarans if she can. Good thinkin', Phyl."

"Thanks, Ben. What are you guys doing?"

"We're headed out to explore the caves where my mom found the ancient spaceship. We would have invited you along, but Sam said you wouldn't want to miss your lunch date."

"She's right about that. You guys have fun," Phyl said. "Call when you get back to the city."

While I was talking to Phyl, we'd left the city behind and were now in a desolate area of desert, rocky spires, and mesas. It reminded me of pictures I'd seen of New Mexico on Earth. "Have they built a visitor's center or anything out here?" I asked.

"No. We've erected some monuments and put up some plagues to explain the significance of what happened here, but the area is very remote and doesn't attract many visitors. Most Sandaarans and travelers are happy to see the museum exhibit and leave it at that."

"I seem to remember that there were some Sandaarans who weren't happy to have this part of their history exposed. Is that still an issue?" I asked.

"Maybe a little bit. There are still those who would like to see Sandaara return to our isolationist ways."

"Are you one of them?"

"Definitely not. I think most of the younger generations are happy that we have a larger universe to explore. It's still true that very few of us travel off this planet, but most of us hope to have the chance someday. We enjoy the changes tourism and trade have brought to our world."

"Since you're a local, what did you think of Detective Lurance?" I asked, earning me a raised eyebrow from Sam. "Do you think he's a good guy?"

After giving me a look similar to Sam's, M'Triska said, "I'm not sure what you mean, but I don't believe the security force is in the habit of hiring the bad guys other than perhaps the occasional informant. Why do you ask?"

"Phyl's like a little sister me," Ben said. "I'm just looking out for her."

"Right," Sam said.

"I had never met the detective until last night, but he seemed genuine enough. Did you get the same vibe, Sam?"

"Yes. I'm sure Phyl will have a pleasant lunch. She'll probably teach the detective more than he ever wanted to learn about fake artifacts."

CHAPTER THIRTEEN

We all settled into our own thoughts for a bit, enjoying the scenery. I was trying to decide how to tell my mom I was turning down the Sandaaran job without telling her what I planned to do instead. I knew she'd prefer that any job I took kept me closer to home. Now, that she's the Chancellor of the Tralaskan council, she and Dad spend most of their time on Tralaska. I knew she'd like nothing better than for me to take a job on Tralaska, but she was smart enough to know that wouldn't be my first choice. Although Sandaara was one of the League's most remote planets, I think she found it an acceptable choice because she had ties there. Of course, I'd have a tough time finding any planet or station in the League that one of my parents didn't have some tie to.

"M'Triska, does this road get much traffic?" Sam asked.

"No. Not many people travel out into the desert."

"I think there's a vehicle following us," Sam said.

I straightened up in my seat and turned to look behind us. There was another vehicle that did seem to be following us, but there weren't a lot of roads.

"Sorry," M'Triska said. "I should have told you. They are following us. It's a media crew. They want to film Ben exploring the spaceship his parents found."

"Great," I said. "And I thought we were just going to have a quiet day hiking in the desert."

"It'll be fun," Sam said. "Your mom will love it, Ben."

She was right about that. I'd just have to find a way to use it to my advantage. "M'Triska, how did you decide to work for the government?" I asked.

"All of my family are government workers. I always knew it's what I would do."

"See that's the problem," I said, turning around to face Sam and Rufus. "So many of the species of the league do what's expected. It sets an ugly precedent."

"Maybe we've been thinking about this the wrong way," Rufus said. "Instead of thinking about the kind of jobs we can get, maybe we need to think about starting our own business."

"That would be great," Sam said. "We need to find something that will make money and let us work together."

"Yeah, that'll be much easier to figure out," I said, unable to shake my sour mood.

I thought it was sweet that M'Triska laid a comforting hand on my thigh, but at the moment, I wasn't in the right frame of mind to enjoy it. I sulked until M'Triska stopped the vehicle next to a small habitat module.

"I have the keys to the hab module," M'Triska said. "We can freshen up inside before we head into the caverns."

We grabbed our packs and followed M'Triska inside. When I came out of the men's room, M'Triska took my arm and led me over to a group of Sandaarans who must have come from the vehicle that followed us. "This is Ben Thurgood, son of Dr. Nebulon Blyst and Viscount Jason Thurgood."

Way to help me forget the expectations I had to live up to, I thought. I answered their questions as best I could while waiting for Rufus and Sam to be ready to go.

"I'm anxious to see these caves. If everyone's ready, let's hit the trail," I said when I saw Rufus help Sam with her pack.

"Why the sudden enthusiasm?" Sam asked quietly enough that only I could hear.

"There's not much hope of ditching the press out here. I'm just trying to make the best of it. I'm thinking I can tell my mom I turned down the job because everything I tried to do would be turned into a media circus. I think there's a chance she'll buy that. She's no big fan of the media."

"Whatever lets you sleep at night," she said, dropping back to walk beside Rufus.

I have to admit, the cave paintings were pretty awesome, and it was cool knowing that my mom was the major reason anyone knew they existed let alone what they meant. I love my folks, and I'm proud of all their accomplishments, but it's a tough act to follow sometimes. In my current state of trying to figure out what to do with my life, I can admit that I'm afraid nothing I do could possibly measure up to the legends my parents have become.

"You OK, Ben?" Sam asked, slipping her arm around my shoulders.

"Yeah, fine. This just reminds me how impossible it is for me or anyone to measure up to my parents. They're legends of the League."

"They are that," she said. "You know, maybe that makes it easier."

I gave her a puzzled look.

"If you know you can't measure up, then you're free to find your own path."

Sam always had a unique way of interpreting things, but maybe she was right. If I could admit I'd never be as legendary as my folks, then maybe I could just figure out what would make me happy.

CHAPTER FOURTEEN

"I'm heading out to lunch, Out," Phyl said.

"Have fun. I understand you have a date with a detective."

"That's true." It really hadn't hit Phyl until this morning that she had a date. A real date. With a handsome, older guy. Older, but maybe not too much. He was nice looking and interesting. She was excited to have a date, but not as excited as she thought she would be. She spent a good long time analyzing why that was before she realized there was no spark. She always assumed that romantic attractions made themselves known by some sort of electrical chemistry between the two parties. She liked Tren well enough and thought he was nice looking, but there was no spark as far as she could tell.

Spark or not, she planned to enjoy her lunch. "I'll check in if I decide to go anywhere after lunch."

"Excellent," Out said.

She chose to dress more conservatively today, wearing comfortable jeans and another from her large collection of pink kitty t-shirts. She spotted Tren waiting for her. As she approached, he got a strange look on his face. "Hi, Tren," she said. "Is something wrong?"

"No. Sorry. Hi, Ophyllia. How are you today?"

"I'm fine. You look like something's bothering you. Has there been some new development with the case?"

"No. It's just, you look younger today."

"I guess I should have dressed differently," she said. "I'm as old as I was yesterday. In fact, I'm older. So how old are you, Tren?"

"I'm 21. How old are you?"

Deftly deflecting his query, she said, "I'm finishing my last year at LSI, the same as Ben and the rest of my friends." She knew he was likely to have some idea how old Ben was, and she was hoping he'd leave it at that. "Where are we having lunch? I'm starved."

He took her hand and walked to a bridge that crossed to the opposite side of the civic pools. "This is one of my favorite places. We call it grab and go food. I thought we could find a table on the esplanade where we could eat and talk."

While they ate lunch, Tren shared what information he'd learned about the people Phyl identified as being involved in the plot at the museum. "I checked into all three of them. None of them have anything criminal in their backgrounds. They all have strong work histories. It seems unlikely they'd do anything to put their jobs at risk."

"They're involved. Maybe some of them are being forced to play a part in the switch, but they are definitely involved. Whether it's by choice or not is something you'll have to figure out."

"I'll do my best. Where are your friends today?"

"They're taking a tour of the caves Ben's mom discovered before he was born."

"Do you know if they plan to visit the spaceship crash site?"

"They didn't mention it. Should I text them not to miss it?"

"No. M'Triska will make sure they see all the important stuff. I'll be right back," he said, and headed off toward the restrooms, but Phyl noticed he changed direction and headed to the other side of the bar where a guy in a dark hoodie was standing. Phyl thought it looked like the guy from the museum tour. She assumed maybe it was another undercover officer.

When Tren returned to the table, he said, "If you're finished eating, I'd like to get your statement recorded. We can do it here, if that's OK with you, or I can take you to the station."

"Was that another undercover officer you were talking to?" Phyl asked.

"I wasn't talking to anyone," he said. "Now, let's get your statement on the record?"

"Here's fine by me," Phyl said. "I'd like to get a cold glass of water before we get started."

"Sure. I'll go get us some drinks. I'll be right back," he said, giving her shoulder a squeeze as he walked off.

When Tren returned he set the drinks on the table and put a small recorder on the table between them. After recording the particulars of names and dates, Tren said, "Just tell me everything that happened on your tour of the museum yesterday afternoon in as much detail as you can remember."

Phyl retold the story from the time she met the tour group until she met up with Detective Lurance outside the museum. He didn't interrupt her, but after she finished, he asked her some questions. Other than the conclusions she'd already drawn about those involved, she couldn't see that they learned anything more from recounting what happened.

"I am curious about something," Tren said. "When you visited the museum exhibits, do you remember seeing anything that you thought might be a fake?"

"Not that I noticed, but then I wasn't expecting to find fakes in the museum at that point. If I went back again, I might find something."

"You won't be going back, because it's not safe," Tren said. "We'll have to get someone to examine everything. We need to figure out how long this has been going on and how much of what's on display is not authentic. This could be a big scandal for the museum."

"I'm not sure how much you know about Ben's background."

"Quite a lot, actually. Its required reading for young Sandaarans. I think our parents' generation was a little embarrassed that an outsider had to expose our history."

"Before Ben's mom visited Sandaara, she and Mr. Thurgood were involved in stopping the sale of artifacts on the black market. Ben said you could message him if you want him to contact his mom to see if she still has any connections that might help you with this case."

"That's terrific. I just might do that," Tren said. "This has been great, but I have to get back to work. Thank you for all of your help with this."

"Thanks for lunch. I'm glad I could help," Phyl said.

"Stay out of trouble," Tren said as they headed in opposite directions on the esplanade.

CHAPTER FIFTEEN

After hiking through the caves and making frequent stops to examine the cave paintings which were now protected by a weatherproof sealant, I was ready to head back. "We're almost to the main attraction," M'Triska said, taking my hand and pulling me forward. We stepped out into an oasis of greenery. Plants grew everywhere, and I could hear the sound of running water.

"This is the spaceship from Tralaska that crashed here. It is perhaps the single most important artifact of the history of my people, and we wouldn't have it had your parents not taken an interest in our planet."

"I'm starting to think you're only interested in me because of my folks."

"They saved my species from a lonely and limited existence," M'Triska said. "They are revered here. Is that such a bad thing?"

"No. Of course not," Ben said. "My dad built a model of this scene. He's really into spaceships." Ben went up to take a closer look. Something wasn't right. "Can we go inside?"

"Sure, just be careful," M'Triska said.

"Have you ever been inside?" Ben asked.

"No. It's not allowed."

"But you said it's OK for me to go in?" I questioned.

"Sure, you're Ben Thurgood."

I looked over my shoulder and saw the grin on Sam's face. "Go ahead. We wouldn't know what we were looking at anyway."

I stuck my head inside and looked around. My dad had all kinds of pictures of the craft that he felt sure had been piloted by one of his ancestors. It was a bit of a family heirloom in some ways, I guess. I knew the minute I looked inside that something was wrong.

"M'Triska, who's responsible for securing this site?" I asked. I had seen no sign of any security presence. It was a remote site which made it more secure in some ways and put it at greater risk in others.

"Sandaaran Security is responsible. I'm not sure what they actually do. I've only been out here a few times, and I've never seen any security officers. I guess because it's so remote, there's really not much chance of problems."

"I'm sorry to tell you this, but the inside of the ship has been vandalized and some, if not all, of the ship's shell has been switched."

"You must be mistaken, Ben," M'Triska said.

"Ben's never wrong about spaceships," Rufus said, joining the discussion.

"My dad had tons of pictures of the inside of this ship. It's been gutted. Maybe they removed it to put it on display somewhere," I suggested. "That would explain it."

"I haven't heard of that, but I'll check."

"Could they have removed the whole ship and replaced it with this empty shell?" Ruf asked.

"I guess it's possible. I just can't see why anyone would bother."

"Ben, I need your help," M'Triska said. "We need to ask the media people not to publish this part of the story."

I went with M'Triska to talk with the media while Sam and Rufus photographed the ship. "Let's head back to the vehicle," M'Triska said when we walked back to the ship. "I need to make some calls."

There really was no way to rush back. It took several hours to get back to the parking area. As we walked, we talked through possible explanations for what we saw at the ship. We all hoped the government had removed the ship to display it at the museum, but somehow, I knew that wasn't the case.

As we neared the vehicle, M'Triska said, "Ben, am I correct that your experience as a pilot also means you can drive most any conveyance?"

"I can drive while you make calls," I said.

"We may not have connection for a while, but I want to draft the messages so they're delivered as soon as possible. I'm also going to ask that security agents or the military are sent to guard the site so there's no further damage."

"Sounds like a plan." As we drove, I dictated a message to my father.

By the time, we reached the city limits, we were scheduled to meet Councilor Dram in his office. As we walked into the building, Rufus asked, "Do you think this could have been done by the same people who are switching artifacts at the museum?"

"I guess it's possible," I said as we picked up our visitor badges and boarded the lift.

Dram himself was waiting for us when the doors opened on the fifteenth floor. "I'm glad to see you again so soon, Ben, though I'm sorry for the circumstances."

Once we were all seated around the conference room table, I introduced my friends and explained what I'd discovered at the site.

"Are you sure?" Dram asked.

"Yes, sir." I pulled up some photos I had taken of the ship earlier in the day. "If you can pull up any photos you have of the find, you'll see the difference."

Dram opened his datapad and brought up the photos. Displayed side-by-side on the room's projection screen it was easy to see the differences.

"Oh, dear. This is not good," Dram said.

We talked about what the security set up was at the site and how we could go about learning when the switch had been made. "I need time to gather some information," Dram said. "Could you all meet me back here tomorrow morning?"

"Certainly, sir. We're happy to help," I said.

Before we got back into the vehicle, I said, "M'Triska do you mind if I have a word with my friends. We need to make some plans." She got in the vehicle to wait for us.

"I'd rather be on the ship. We have more resources to help us figure this out," I said. "Do you two mind if I have M'Triska drop me off at the spaceport. She can take you two back to the resort to get our stuff and then drive you back to the ship."

"Sounds like a plan," Rufus said.

CHAPTER SIXTEEN

"Hi, Honey. I'm home." I called as I entered the Screamer. "Welcome back, Ben," Out said.

"Is Phyl here?"

"She's been in her room for several hours. I'm not sure what she's doing, but she's been using a lot of computing cycles."

"Good to know," I said and knocked on the door of Phyl's cabin. She didn't answer, so I knocked again. "Phyl, it's Ben. Are you OK?"

In a minute, the door opened. "Sorry, Ben. I got absorbed in a project. I looked around the room. Every wall was covered with paper. "Looks like if you're going to be a frequent flyer with us, we'll need to install some note boards in here. And everywhere..."

"Sorry. While I was giving my statement to Tren, I had a great idea. I've been working on it ever since, but what are you doing here?"

"It is my ship."

"I know, but I didn't expect you back tonight. Is everyone here?"

"Not yet. Sam and Ruf went to pick up our gear from the resort. They'll be here shortly. Can you join us in the lounge when they get back?"

"Sure. Are we leaving early?"

"No. I'll fill you in when they get back. So, what's this new thing you're working on?"

"I'll tell everyone about it when we all get together. I just need a few minutes to finish what I was doing."

"I'll knock when they get here."

I took a quick shower and changed into comfy sweats and a t-shirt. I felt like we needed to figure out what was going on, even though I knew Sam would say we should let the authorities handle it. Maybe she was right, but I had to wonder how long the switch would have gone unnoticed if I hadn't visited the site of the crash.

My comm unit bleeped just as I walked into the galley. "Go for Ben."

"Ben, it's Sam. I'm in my room. I just wanted to check with you and see if we should include M'Triska or not when we get back to the ship."

"Sure. Invite her in for the discussion. I can't see any way that she's involved, and we might need a Sandaaran to run interference for us."

"Figured you'd say that. You know we could just give a report and let the authorities handle it."

"Figured you'd say that. Get your butts back here so we can figure this out."

"Yes sir, Captain, sir. On our way."

XXX

By the time Rufus, Sam, and M'Triska walked into the Screamer, I had grabbed a selection of snacks from the galley and moved an extra chair in from my cabin. The Screamer was a small ship. There were four passenger cabins and a shared galley/lounge area in addition to the cockpit and a small cargo bay. Normally, it was just me or Sam, Rufus, and me. Now, with Phyl on board and M'Triska joining us for the discussion, it was starting to feel a little crowded.

I explained what I'd seen at the crash site. From what I could tell, none of the cave paintings had been damaged. All the other pottery shards and artifacts found in the caves had been moved to the museum years ago. Only the paintings were preserved and left in place. At the crash site, the ship had been left as it was found with only a plague added to explain the significance. I recapped our meeting with Dram. "Have you heard anything more, M'Triska?"

"No. I suspect it will be morning before I get any more information from Councilor Dram."

Phyl listened carefully to my story but said nothing. It wasn't like her not to burst into the conversation with a million questions. I looked at her and could almost see the gears in her brain turning. "Phyl, what are you thinking?"

"I need to explain what I was working on today," she said. "It's a long story, but I think it has something to do with what you found at the crash site."

It took a while for all of us to understand what Phyl had done, but once she showed us, it clicked...mostly. She realized when she gave her statement to Tren, that she was basically describing everything she could remember about what happened. She decided to use technology to create a vid from her description that would allow her to playback what she saw. She pulled in every possible video feed to use in making her crime scene vid as she called it. She took footage from the lobby of the museum which showed the tour group and was able to use that to make a video representation of the scene in the lab. It was pretty complicated, but the gist of it was that we could now watch a video of what her statement was describing.

"That way, I can watch it like a movie and maybe see things I left out or remember something. It would also be able to combine multiple witness statements into one view," she said.

"That's really cool, Phyl,"

"Thanks. I think I might be able to sell this to security agencies. With some more work, it could be used to turn any witness statement into a video of their recollection of a crime."

"Way to go," Sam said, giving Phyl a high five.

"Let me show you what I realized," Phyl said, playing the video on the big view screen in the lounge. She fast forwarded to the lab scene. "Pay attention to this guy over here," she said, pointing to a young guy wearing a hoodie, "and Tren." She forwarded through the video again until she was seated outside the museum sipping a drink. She stopped the video again. "This is where Tren went to get a drink."

"Is that the guy from the tour?"

"Yep. He said something to Tren. It could be harmless, but I don't think so. Today Tren asked me where you guys were. When I told him you were going to tour the caves, he asked if you were going to the crash site. I said I didn't know. He brushed the comment aside, but immediately sent a text message. A few minutes later while I was giving my statement, he stopped the recording and excused himself to go to the restroom. I noticed he didn't go the right way. He went around the other side of the bar and talked to that guy again."

"You're sure?"

"I'm sure. When I asked him about it, he got all weirded out and denied it. He rushed me to get through my statement and then couldn't get back to work soon enough."

CHAPTER SEVENTEEN

The group lapsed into a discussion about how likely it was that the museum incident and the spaceship situation were related. We all agreed that it sounded like Detective Lurance was involved. We took a break to get drinks and snacks before trying to figure out what our next steps should be.

Before we resumed, my comm unit bleeped. "Hi, Dad. How are you and Mom?"

"Your Mom's been tied up in meetings all day, as usual. I'm really upset about what's happened on Sandaara. Have you reported it to the authorities?"

"Yeah. I went to Councilor Dram. Do you remember Phyl Devlin?"

"Sure. She's your classmate from LSI and a relative of Ciara."

"She came along on this trip and earlier she toured the museum and found that some of the artifacts there have been switched for fakes. We're thinking it's all tied together."

"Any idea who's behind it?"

"We've identified three people involved at the museum and one detective on the Sandaaran Security Force."

"Good work, son. I'm proud of you. Your mom will be too. What can I do to help?"

"I know you guys used to work on this kind of stuff. I thought you might still have some contacts that could find out who would be interested in buying that spaceship and have the money to pay for it. I'm thinking Tralaskan, but you and Mom are the experts on this stuff."

"I'll look into it. Be careful, Ben."

"Sure thing, Dad. Give my love to Mom."

We all wanted to find a way to catch those involved. We discussed lots of idea but didn't come up with anything we thought was relatively foolproof. Finally, about 2:00 AM, we came up with a plan we thought was likely to be successful and pose little risk to any of us.

We decided to sleep on it. We'd see if we all still agreed in the morning. I walked M'Triska to her vehicle and headed back to the Screamer. I felt like someone was watching me, but I didn't see anyone. I called M'Triska as soon as I got back aboard."

"Miss me already?" she asked.

"No. I think someone was watching us when I walked you out. I just wanted to warn you to be cautious."

XXX

By the time I woke up, I had messages from M'Triska, my mom, my dad, and Councilor Dram. I decided all of them could wait until I had a shower and a cup of coffee. I'm not a great morning person.

Dad's message said he was looking into the people most likely to have purchased the crashed spaceship on the black market. He'd already made his connections at the Cube and OffSec aware of what we found.

Mom's message said she was proud of me but didn't want me to put myself in a dangerous situation. It ended with "I know you're your father's son, but remember he had a Tyen around to protect him." Yeah along with being a legendary xenoarchaeologist and politician, my mother is also a Tyen—she can change into a Tralaskan warrior woman. It's something to do with recessive genes and threats to Tralaska, but it makes my mother one of the most feared beings in the League, yet another reason I have to think carefully about my choices.

M'Triska's message just said she was safe and to let her know what time to pick us up.

Dram wanted to meet with us at 11AM. He suggested it might be best if he came to us.

When I walked out of my cabin, Rufus and Sam were in the galley cooking breakfast. "Good, I waited long enough. I see you already made coffee," I said as Sam handed me an empty mug and pointed toward a coffee pot on the table. "We need to eat and clean up. Councilor Dram is coming here at 11:00 AM."

"Anything I can do?" Out asked.

"Just record everything while he's here. I trust him, but I want to make sure we cover all our bases. Is Phyl up yet?"

"I haven't seen her, but I heard noises from her cabin," Sam said.

"Do you think she can handle this?" I asked.

"Yes, I can handle it," she said, walking through the outside hatch. She was dressed in a mechanic's onesy that was covered in grease stains and had a cap pulled down over her face.

"Where have you been?"

"Seeing if we had any watchers on us."

"Out, why didn't you tell me Phyl had gone out?"

"You didn't ask, Ben."

"There are two guys with eyes on the ship, one is cleaning the cleanest spaceport floor I've ever seen, just outside the hatch. The other, is in the arrivals hall."

"What makes you think they're watching us?"

"I tagged them. Floor polisher guy hasn't moved from the same 4-foot section of floor in the last hour. If he keeps polishing that same section, he's going to fall through to the lower level. The other guy is definitely watching someone. It's hard to know for sure that's it's us, but we seem to be the most interesting show on Sandaara, so I think the odds are in our favor."

I went into my cabin and relayed the information on the two watchers to Councilor Dram. "Do you want me to have security apprehend them?"

"I think it's best if we leave them where they are until we've completed our con."

"OK. See you at 11:00."

CHAPTER EIGHTEEN

"OK, everyone. Last chance. Any questions or second thoughts?"

No one raised any issues. OK. Let's go catch us some bad guys," I said.

The setup of Detective Lurance was part one of our plan. Phyl called the detective and asked that he meet her on the esplanade. "Hi, Phyl," he said as he walked up. "I'm glad I got to see you again."

"I hope you still think so after I explain why I called. Look I know you're involved in the switching of the artifacts at the museum," Phyl said. "Don't bother denying it. I have enough proof to take to OffSec."

"How could you possibly know that?" She was pleased he hadn't tried to deny it.

"I'm a very resourceful girl," she said. "Remember at our lunch date when you thought I was too young."

"In my defense, you looked a lot younger than you did at the museum."

"It doesn't matter. Ben and his friends always treat me like a child, and I'm tired of it. Besides coming for a job interview with your government, Ben is here to present some old pot to Councilor Dram. I don't really know why it's important, and I don't care. I want you to help me steal it and replace it with a fake. I want to show them that they need to take me seriously."

"What's the split on the money from the sale?"

"No split. You can have it all. My family is wealthy. I just want to teach them a lesson."

Whether it was because he was attracted to her, or because he couldn't resist easy money, Tren agreed. He told Phyl she'd need to provide photos of the object so he could get a fake made.

"We have to move fast," she said. "The ceremony is on Friday. We'll need to make the switch before that."

Dram had a small Sandaaran pot pulled from the private collection of a friend. A good quality fake was made, and Phyl sent images of the original to Tren.

Tren messaged Phyl as soon as the fake was ready. They met for drinks and planned to steal the original from the Screamer. "Are you sure there's no onboard security system?"

"Of course there's an onboard security system, but I know how to shut it off. Ben showed me how to override it in case I needed to shut it down in an emergency."

"Will any of your friends be able to tell it's not real?"

"Not if your people making the copy are any good," she said. "They're not as smart as I am."

"OK. I'll let you know when I have the copy."

XXX

Phyl returned to the Screamer after doing some shopping in town. They were trying to make everything look as normal as possible. "You did good, Phyl," Sam said. "Any problems?"

"The hardest part was not being offended that he thought I'd actually do something like this and just not disabling him with my blaster pen."

"What's this about a blaster pen?" Rufus asked.

"We'll talk later," Phyl said, patting his arm. "After dealing with that slime ball, I need a shower."

CHAPTER NINETEEN

While they waited for Phyl to get the call that Tren had the fake artifact, they planned the final two stages of the operation. Ben's parents had contacted Dram directly and were working to identify others involved in the sale of the stolen artifacts from Sandaara. With the help of OffSec, they added several names to the list of suspects.

"Tren just called," Phyl said as she walked into the lounge. "He has the fake. I'm supposed to let him know when you're gone."

"I'll notify Dram."

About an hour later, there was a knock on the hatch, "Pizza delivery," the guy called.

Once the pizza delivery guy was inside, he stripped off his uniform and handed it to Phyl. We made sure to find someone who was similar in size. This was our way to get Phyl off the Screamer without raising suspicions. She headed back to the spaceport pizza shop to change out of the uniform and settled in to wait. She argued that it would be easier if she stayed on the ship, but I wouldn't allow it.

Once Phyl was gone and the OffSec agent was on the Screamer, Rufus, Sam, and I headed out. The two watchers had acquired watchers of their own. The OffSec agent sent a message from Phyl's communicator saying she was alone on the ship and had set the override on the Screamer's security system. Tren said he'd give the agreed to signal when he was at the hatch.

We headed out of the spaceport and got into M'Triska's vehicle. "Where to?" she asked."

"I don't want to go far, but we need to make it look like were leaving," I said.

"Got it," she pulled away and headed out along the main highway.

"Where are we going?" I asked.

"Does it matter?"

"I guess not," I said. I was anxious to get word that Tren Lurance had been taken into custody. I could only hope that Phyl would stick to the plan and sit tight at the pizza place. I wished I could check on her, but she had to leave her communicator with the OffSec agent on the Screamer.

No one talked much as M'Triska drove. We were all in our own heads, just waiting to get word that the operation had gone as planned. As soon as Tren made his way into the Screamer, each of the watcher's we identified would be apprehended. Several spaceport workers transporting goods and servicing ships had been replaced with undercover OffSec agents who would move in to surround the Screamer and apprehend Tren.

M'Triska pulled us into an underground garage. "Just sit tight. We're out of sight here," she said.

"What's in this building?" I asked.

"There are several shops, restaurants, and businesses as well as some apartments on the higher floors."

"Great. If anyone is watching, it would make sense for us to be here."

I leaned back in my seat and closed my eyes. Waiting was much more difficult than taking action. M'Triska rested her hand on my thigh. "I'm going to stand outside and make a call. I'll be right back. Just relax."

When my door opened a few minutes later, I assumed it was M'Triska until I felt the blaster pushed into my ribs.

"What the...?"

"Shut up. Get out of the vehicle very slowly." The voice was male but that was all I could make out. When I stepped down out of the vehicle, I saw Rufus and Sam both with their hands cuffed in front of them. M'Triska was holding a blaster on Sam while there was a man on each side of Rufus both pointing blasters at his head. "M'Triska, what's going on?"

"Ben, are you shocked to find out that I'm not your biggest fan? Sorry. Please just do as we say, and no one will get hurt." She motioned me into an elevator with two other men with blasters.

"What about them?" I said, nodding toward Sam and Rufus.

"They'll be joining us upstairs." The elevator doors closed and M'Triska said "twenty-five".

I didn't put up a fight. It would have been pointless. It wasn't easy to bide my time, but I knew Sam, Rufus, and I together could get out of anything. I was seated on a plush sofa and one of the guards removed the handcuffs, and replaced them around my left hand, attaching it to metal arm of the sofa. I pulled just to test it. Of course, it felt secure. The door opened, and a guard walked in carrying Sam fireman style over one shoulder with her butt facing upward. I guess she hadn't decided to go quietly. "Put me down, you idiot. I can walk. What the ..."

"Hi, Sam. Have a seat," I said. Patting the sofa beside me. She stared at me like I'd told her to eat her socks or something. "We're out manned and out gunned," I said. "No sense fighting it, right now." I gave her a look which I hoped she understood meant that I wasn't giving up, I was just waiting and trying to figure a way out that wouldn't get any of us killed.

The door opened and the guard holding on to one of Rufus' arms, walked in pulling Rufus after him. "Cooperate, Ruf," I shouted. I needed my friend to be unharmed if I wanted to use his strength to escape later.

The guards cuffed Sam to my right arm and then repeated the same scenario with Rufus. All three of us were cuffed together, and Rufus and I were cuffed to the sofa arms.

"You guys OK?" I asked as two guards pulled up chairs to sit in front of us. Rufus nodded, and Sam gave me an eye roll. "Seems we must have overlooked one background check," I said, nodding my head toward the kitchen, where M'Triska was on her communicator.

As soon as she ended her call, she looked me in the eye. I had the impression she was trying to communicate something, but the message was definitely not received.

"Guys, give me a couple of minutes. I want to make sure they realize just how much trouble they're in. They're all really smart, aren't you?" she asked, looking at us. "Aren't you?" We all nodded our heads in the affirmative.

The guards grumbled a bit but left when M'Triska motioned them out with her blaster.

"Now which of you is the best actor?" she asked before the door closed behind the guards.

CHAPTER TWENTY

Phyl had been waiting in the back of the pizza place so long she was thinking about helping them make the pizzas just to pass the time. Ben was supposed to come get her as soon as Tren was in custody. Something must have gone wrong. Every few minutes she thought about heading back to the Screamer, but she talked herself into staying put.

Finally, an elderly Sandaaran walked into the kitchen followed by two men who appeared to be security guards. "Ms. Devlin, it's me, Councilor Dram. Until we're sure what's going on, they won't let me ditch the disguise."

"What happened?" Phyl asked.

"We got Tren. That part went off without a hitch. OffSec is interrogating him now. We're hopeful that he'll give us the names of all of those involved."

"Great, then I can go back to the Screamer," Phyl said, standing up.

"We'll escort you," Dram said as he and his security guards followed her through the spaceport back to the bay where the Screamer was docked. The hatch was open, and Phyl rushed in. "I'm so glad you're all..." She looked around. There was no one there.

"Where is everyone?"

"Sit down, Ms. Devlin. We need to talk."

As he explained, Phyl's head fell onto her arms which were crossed in front of her on the table. When he finished, she picked her head up. "M'Triska is in on this, and she's taken Ben, Rufus, and Sam. Don't you guys vet your employees? I thought she worked for the Sandaaran government."

"She does. Please let me finish. She works for us, but she's been undercover for months infiltrating the crime family behind this. We weren't sure they were involved until Ben's father turned up some compelling evidence implicating them."

Phyl's head had fallen onto her arms again. She turned it to the side to look at Dram. "What's going on? Make it simple, please?"

"Why Ms. Devlin, with your IQ, you should have already figured it out, but perhaps your hormones got in the way."

"Excuse me," Phyl said, standing up from her chair. "Did you just blame my lack of understanding on hormones." Her voice had risen to an ear-splitting level.

"Ms. Ophyllia, are you OK?" Out asked.

"I'm fine, Out. OK. So M'Triska and her goons who aren't really her goons have taken my three friends hostage or something. Can she get them out? Is it possible that she's been compromised? Do you know where they are at this moment? Do you have a plan to rescue them or shall I use my exceptional IQ to figure that out for myself too?"

"I'm sorry, Ms. Devlin. My comments were inappropriate. I'm just concerned. We never intended to put any of you in harm's way, least of all Ben."

"So, if I was kidnapped, you'd feel better about it, but since they've got Ben you're upset. Geez, you guys take this hero worship thing a bit too far. Sit," she said, motioning Dram to a chair. His security guards watched her nervously, but Dram waved them off.

"Let's go through the important stuff one thing at a time. Do you know where they are?"

"I believe I do."

"Then why aren't we currently on our way to their location? Have you sent in a rescue team?"

"Not yet. M'Triska has a plan. I agreed to let her do things her way."

"What can I do?"

"Calm down and wait."

"Neither of those is likely to happen for long," Phyl said, walking into her cabin and closing the door behind her.

"Out. We need to figure out how to save Ben, Sam, and Rufus."

"I have their location."

"Get me any information on the location."

"Will do. Councilor Dram and his guards are still sitting in the lounge."

"Good. Keep an eye and ear on them. Get me every scrap of data you can find on M'Triska."

After sitting in the small lounge area of the Screamer for a few minutes, one of the guards leaned over and said, "Councilor, I don't think she's coming back. What should we do?"

"We wait. I have a feeling we shouldn't leave Ms. Devlin unsupervised."

After a few minutes, Phyl rushed into the lounge and asked, "Can you get someone to fly me to the top of the building where they're being held?"

"Ms. Devlin, I'm not sure..." Dram started to say.

"Can you?"

"We can." he said, and she went back to her cabin and closed the door again.

"Sir, do you think that's wise?" one of the guards asked.

"I said that we can. I didn't say that we would."

CHAPTER TWENTY-ONE

"Do we trust her?" Sam whispered in my ear.

"We don't have much choice. What do you think?"

"You're right. There's no other option. Just do it," she said.

I looked over her shoulder, and Rufus nodded his agreement. If I had other choices, I wouldn't have trusted M'Triska, but we had no options. I hoped Phyl was safe. I knew she'd be worried when I didn't show up to retrieve her from her hiding place in the pizza place's kitchen. I hoped Dram or someone figured out what happened and was mounting a rescue. In the meantime, I hoped my slim faith in M'Triska hadn't been misplaced. In the few moments, she was alone with us, she told us she was an agent working undercover for the government. She infiltrated the gang behind the artifact thefts but needed more time to get to the top people behind the operation. With Dram's approval, she was basically using me as bait. I wasn't really happy about that, though I guess I should feel honored that she thought the top bad guy would put in an appearance for me.

We didn't have time to discuss a plan but were following her lead as best we could. She circled the sofa, checking us each out like we were pieces of cake in a bakery window. "Sit," she told the two guards, motioning to the chairs facing us. "The boss won't be here for a while, so I'm going to have some fun." She dropped into Ruf's lap and ran her hand down his jaw. Then she squeezed his bicep. Her act was so over the top that I had to bite my tongue to keep from laughing, but Rufus seemed to be enjoying it.

She stood up and walked behind the sofa. She lifted Sam's hair and let it fall through her fingers. "You and I could have some fun trading makeup tips and doing each other's hair, but that's not what I'm in the mood for tonight."

I had a feeling I knew what was coming, but all I could do was play along. M'Triska perched on the sofa arm beside me and stroked my forearm. "I do like this one, but he hasn't been very cooperative. Perhaps now that I'm in charge, you'll see things my way. Cuff his hands and restrain these two. After the guard cuffed my hands in front of me, M'Triska wrapped her arms around my bicep and pulled me toward a closed door. Inside was a nice bedroom and a private bath.

"What..." She pressed her finger to my lips to keep me quiet. She pulled me into the bathroom and turned on the fan. She rifled through the drawer and pulled out a small device. She pushed a button, and my cuffs released falling into her hand. She laid them on the counter. "We need to make a plan to get free?" I asked.

"Yes and no. You have to be here when the boss arrives. We need to arrest him."

"Won't he bring more guards with him?"

"Probably, but we can deal with that. She pulled a small bottle out of the top drawer and shook out four pills. She filled a glass with water and swallowed one of the pills. She handed the glass and a pill to me. "This will keep us safe when I release the gas."

"What gas?" I asked.

"The apartment is rigged with anesthesia gas. It will incapacitate all those not protected." She handed the two remaining pills to me. Get your friends to take these as soon as you can after we go back out there. It takes a while for it to kick in."

"How do you release the gas?"

"I'll take care of that."

"And if you're unavailable, I want to have the option."

We stared each other down, but neither of us blinked. "Do you know how the gas or the antidote affects different species?"

She grinned. "It's a little late to ask that now, isn't it?"

"Better late than never. Has it been tested on various species?"

"Yes. As long as the boss isn't Martok, we should be fine."

"You've never seen him or her?"

"Him, I think. No. I've talked to him on the comm."

"Could I have a minute?" I asked, motioning to the bathroom.

She walked out and left me to do what I needed to do. I left the water running and opened the drawer. I took the cuff release and tucked it in my pocket. I hoped she wouldn't notice, or if she did, she wouldn't care.

When I walked out, she stood up. "We need to make this believable." She threw her head back and laughed. She put her arms around my neck and pulled me close, kissing me in a way that felt way too real for me. "Come on, Ben. At least act like you're enjoying it a little."

"Sorry," I whispered in her ear. "Nothing about this situation is enjoyable. I want my friends out of danger."

At that point, I heard a crash from the other room. "What the ..." I yelled as I headed for the door forgetting I wasn't cuffed.

I heard M'Triska, say "Plark" and follow me out. It took a moment for me to take it all in. Phyl was standing there pointing a blaster at one of the guards, one guard laid unconscious or dead on the floor in front of a broken window surrounded by glass. Two others were being subdued by what I thought were members of Sandaaran special forces based on their uniforms.

Ruf and Sam still sat cuffed on the sofa. I pulled out the device and released their cuffs.

"What the heck happened here?" M'Triska asked. "We need to clean this up. The boss will be here any minute. We need to arrest him."

"There's no time to discuss this. Everyone's OK. Let's just do what needs to be done to put an end to this," Sam said. "Drag the bodies into the bedroom. Can we use these two," she pointed to the spec ops guys, "as stand-ins for the guards?"

"Should work," M'Triska said. "Ben, you three get back on the sofa. Phyl take the cuff release from Ben and hide in the bedroom.

M'Triska swept up the broken glass and closed the curtains which hid the broken window. There was a breeze billowing the curtains, but by the time the guy was far enough into the room to notice, we'd have him.

Once we were all back to waiting, M'Triska said, "He'll probably have two guards with him."

"We'll take care of them," one of the spec ops guys said.

"Phyl, release the cuffs once the guards are down."

"Got it," she called from the bedroom.

When the door alarm sounded, M'Triska took a deep breath and walked to the door. "Where are they?" the Sokuhl said, pushing his way into the room.

"Ah, Benjamin Thurgood. It's good to finally meet you. Your parents have cost me billions of credits over the years. I'm looking forward to extracting my revenge."

As expected, he was followed by two guards. "Good work, M'Triska. I didn't think you were up to the task. I'm glad you proved me wrong."

Ben noticed that M'Triska had made her way behind the sofa, carefully staying out of the man's reach. "Who are your friends?" he asked, looking Ben in the eye.

"I didn't catch your name," I said.

"Forgive me. I'm called Brul. Did your folks ever mention me? It's been a few years since our paths crossed, but I think I made a lasting impression. Now, who are your friends?" he asked, moving to the end of the sofa and staring down at Rufus.

At that point, his cuffs fell open. Rufus is fast for a big guy. He had Brul in a headlock before the rest of us even realized what was happening. At the same time, the spec ops guys took down the guards.

It was all over in a few seconds. M'triska called for backup, while I put in a call to Dram.

CHAPTER TWENTY-TWO

It was a long night. Sandaaran Security took Brul and his crew into custody while M'Triska and the rest of us were transported to Dram's office in the government building. Food and drinks were provided, and we took our seats around the table. "I thought it might be easier if we took your statements in a less formal setting," Dram said. "We all know pieces of the story."

Before we got into the formal statements, I leaned over to Phyl and asked, "How did you end up breaking through the window of an apartment on the twenty-fifth floor with two spec ops guys?"

I guess Dram heard my question. "Ms. Devlin can be incredibly persuasive," he said with a nod to Phyl.

Somehow, Phyl had convinced Dram that she had a device that could stun everyone in the apartment, but she wouldn't allow anyone else to deploy it. She told them it was a prototype and only she could operate the stun bomb.

After they all gave their official statements and answered questions from the security folks and OffSec agents, Dram stood up. "Ben, your parents will be very proud of your actions. You stepped in to help us stop the misappropriation of our artifacts with little regard to your own safety. My thanks go out to all of you. It seems that your family is destined to play a role in Sandaaran society whether official or not. You are all most welcome on Sandaara any time. Ben, I hope that you will give our job offer serious consideration. If any of your friends would like to come here with you, I'm sure we can find positions for all of them."

After handshakes all around, we were driving back to the spaceport. The adrenalin was wearing off, and we were all dragging when we boarded the Screamer.

"Welcome back. Is everyone OK?"

"We're fine, Out. Has it been quiet here?"

"Yes, once Phyl and Councilor Dram departed."

"We were awesome," Phyl said, still wound up from her adventure. "We need to do this kind of stuff. Stop crimes, solve mysteries, do something exciting."

"Slow down, Phyl," I said. "Do you realize how dangerous what you did was? Your folks would never let you put yourself in danger like that."

"I had things under control."

"So, what's this stun bomb, you told Dram about," Sam asked.

Phyl reached into her pocket and pulled out a ping-pong ball sized sphere that had a reflective surface. "This is the prototype."

"You carry a prototype stun bomb around in your pocket?" I asked. "Have you tested it?

"Not yet, but I'm sure it will work."

"So, you were ready to set that thing off in the apartment without knowing whether or not it would kill us all? Geez, Phyl, I thought you liked us," Rufus said.

"It'll work. If it doesn't work, it wouldn't kill you, it just wouldn't stun anyone. I could explain it, but its late and you're all tired."

"Let's call it a night," I said. "I'm beat. We'll head back to LSI tomorrow."

CHAPTER TWENTY-THREE

I was exhausted from all the excitement the day before, but after a good night's sleep and a hot shower, I was ready to get things back to normal. I was relieved that Dram didn't push me to make a decision about the trade attaché position. I needed some time to craft my refusal and prepare my folks.

When I walked out into the lounge, the noteboard on the wall said ORBS drawn in big block letters each a different color. I filled my mug with coffee and sat down to enjoy it. "Out, do you know who wrote this on the noteboard in here?"

"Ms. Ophyllia was up early. I believe she was writing on the noteboard."

"Do you know what it means?"

"I'm not sure what she was working on."

Rufus sat down beside me with his own mug of coffee. "What's that about?" he asked, pointing to the noteboard.

"Not sure. Something Phyl put up there."

"She was sure wound up last night. I can't believe she got to fly with a Sandaaran. That was pretty cool."

"She seems to have no fear or no sense of self-preservation, I'm not sure which."

"Good morning, boys," Sam said, fixing a mug of tea and joining them. "ORBS? Did you finally figure out what you want to do after LSI?"

"Not me. I'm still just as clueless as before we made this trip," I said.

"I wrote that," Phyl said, setting a mug of hot chocolate with big white marshmallows down on the table. "It's ORBS."

"We can see that," Sam said. "What does it mean?"

"It's us," Phyl responded.

We all just nodded and sipped our drinks. No one wanted to ask, but finally I gave in. "OK. We know it says ORBS, but what does that mean?"

"It's us--Ophyllia, Rufus, Ben, and Sam, ORBS. I figured it can be our company name."

"Our company?" Sam asked. "We don't have a company."

"But we can. It's the perfect solution for all of us. We can form a company so we can work together like we did here."

"What will ORBS do?"

"Maybe we can sell some of my inventions, but I'm thinking it'll be a service company. We'll be an expert team fighting crime or solving mysteries or something. "You guys can work out the details, I can't do everything myself. Well I probably could, but I don't want to."

ABOUT JO CAREY

Jo Carey grew up in the Midwest but her curiosity and gypsy-spirit has kept her on the move. She's lived in eight US states and spent three years living in Ireland. She has always loved creature movies, so creatures and bugs often show up in her books.

A former information security compliance guru, Jo writes fast-paced, character-driven science fiction stories. Her tales are filled with humor, romance, and sometimes creatures or aliens, or maybe even all of the above. She often builds her stories around a strong female lead character surrounded by plenty of hunky male heroes.

Jo's been under fire on a golf course and climbed out the roof of an elevator in the Netherlands. Life hasn't been boring. Now residing in Texas, setting often plays a huge role in her stories. Jo was intrigued by the League of Planetary Systems, a world her husband, Frank, created for his science fiction books, and she now writes tales set in that world. Jo was bitten by a cat, a fire ant, and a snake, before succumbing to the bite of the writing bug.

Jo hasn't had personal contact with a cryptid or an alien, but it's never too late.

Jo can be reached via e-mail at elvenindustriespress@gmail.com.
Jo's Amazon Author page:

http://amazon.com/author/jocarey

www.ingramcontent.com/pod-product-compliance
Lightning Source LLC
Chambersburg PA
CBHW020640130626
46552CB00003B/1326

9781948716390